This book belongs to

....

First published in 2014 by Miles Kelly Publishing Ltd
Harding's Barn, Bardfield End Green, Thaxted, Essex, CM6 3PX, UK

2 4 6 8 10 9 7 5 3 1

Publishing Director Belinda Gallagher
Creative Director Jo Cowan
Editor Fran Bromage
Senior Designer Joe Jones
Production Manager Elizabeth Collins
Reprographics Stephan Davis, Jennifer Hunt, Thom Allaway

ISBN 978-1-78209-485-2

Printed in China

British Library Cataloguing-in-Publication Data
A catalogue record for this book is available from the British Library

ACKNOWLEDGEMENTS
The publishers would like to thank the following artists
who have contributed to this book:
Cover (main): Jenny Arthur at The Bright Agency
Insides: Rosalind Beardshaw

Made with paper from a sustainable forest

www.mileskelly.net   info@mileskelly.net

The Ugly Duckling

Miles Kelly

A mother duck was waiting for her eggs to hatch. Slowly, the first shell cracked, and a tiny bill and two yellow wings appeared. With a rush,

The Ugly Duckling

a little yellow duckling fell out. He stretched his wings and began to clean his feathers. Then, he watched his sisters and brothers push their way out of their shells.

Soon there was only one egg left to hatch. It was the

largest, and the mother duck wondered why it was taking so long. She wanted to take her babies for their first swimming lesson.

Suddenly, with a loud crack, there lay the ugliest duckling she had ever seen. He wasn't even yellow — his feathers were grey. "Oh dear," said the mother duck, peering down at the duckling.

She led the family down to the river with the ugly duckling trailing behind. They splashed into the water, and were soon swimming gracefully — except the ugly duckling who looked large and awkward on the water.

"Oh dear," said the mother duck, shaking her head.

The whole family set off for the

The Ugly Duckling

farmyard where they were greeted with hoots and moos and barks and snorts from all the other animals.

"Whatever is that?" said the cockerel, pointing rudely. The other ducklings huddled round their mother and pretended the ugly duckling wasn't with them.

"Oh dear," said the mother duck, waddling away.

The Ugly Duckling

The ugly duckling felt
very sad and lonely. No one
seemed to like him, so he ran
away, and hid in some reeds
by the river.

Some hunters came by with
their noisy guns and big dogs.
The ugly duckling paddled

Story time

The Ugly Duckling

deeper into the thick reeds,
trembling with fear.

All summer he wandered
over fields and down rivers.
Everywhere he went animals
laughed and jeered at him,
and other ducks hissed at
him. The duckling was very

lonely and unhappy. Soon, winter came and the rivers began to freeze over.

One day the duckling found himself trapped in the ice. He wriggled and flapped, but he couldn't get out. He was still there the next morning

The Ugly Duckling

when a farmer came by on his
way to feed his cows.

The farmer broke the ice,
wrapped the ugly duckling
in his jacket and carried him
home to his children. They
put the poor ugly duckling in
a box by the fire, and as he

warmed up they fed him and stroked his feathers. The ugly duckling stayed at the farm through the winter, growing bigger all the time.

Now, the farmer's wife never had much time for the ugly duckling. He was always getting under her feet, and knocking things over. He put his feet in the freshly churned butter and spilt the milk in

the bucket from the cow.

One day the farmer's wife had enough. She chased the ugly duckling right out of the kitchen, out of the farm and down the lane.

It was a perfect spring day. The apple trees were covered

The Ugly Duckling

in blossom and the air was filled with the sound of birdsong. The ugly duckling wandered down to the river, and there he saw three magnificent white swans.

They looked so beautiful and graceful as they glided

towards the bank. He waited for them to hiss at him and beat the water with their wings to frighten him away, but they didn't.

Instead, they called him to come and join them. At first the ugly duckling thought it

The Ugly Duckling

was a joke, but then the
swans asked him again.

So, he bent down to get
into the water, and there
looking back was his own
reflection. But where was the
ugly duckling? All he could
see was a magnificent swan

peering back. He was a swan! Not an ugly duckling, but a beautiful, white swan.

He lifted his long elegant neck, and called out in sheer delight, "I am a SWAN!" and he sailed gracefully over the water to join his real family.

The Ugly Duckling

The End